Grace Anne

Learns to Tell the Truth

Written by Cindy Anne Duncan

Illustrated by Manelle Oliphant

To: Gracey
You are as special
as can be!

Love,
Grace Anne

Good Sound Publishing™

GRACE ANNE LEARNS TO TELL THE TRUTH.
Copyright © 2010 by Good Sound Publishing
Written by Cindy Anne Duncan. Illustrated by Manelle Oliphant.
Edited by Angela Holzer, MA. Front and back cover design by
Manelle Oliphant. Back cover image by Ben Daily. Discussion Page
co-created by Cindy Anne Duncan and Angela Holzer, MA.

All Rights Reserved. Printed in China. No part of this book may
be reproduced or copied in any form without written permission
from the publisher.

For information please address
Good Sound Publishing, Palo Alto CA 94306.

Library of Congress Control Number: 2010926253
ISBN-13: 978-1-935743-00-2

For more information about Good Sound Publishing products,
please visit us at www.GoodSoundPublishing.com

Good Sound Publishing™

This is Grace Anne,
She's special you see,
Most pups have four legs,
But she only has three.

She loves to play and dance
and sing,
But playing with dolls is her most
favorite thing.

Now Grace Anne was extra
excited today,
Because Cousin Emily was
coming to play.

So she dressed herself up with
ribbons and bows,
And polka dots streaming from
head to her toes.

Now since she was ready and
dressed for the day,
She called her friend Nickel who
came over to play.

The two were so busy with all
of their fuss,
They didn't see Emily step
out of the bus.

Emily walked in with her
big bag of toys,
"Let's Play!"
Grace Anne shouted,
while jumping with joy!

"These toys are not yours,"
cried Emily out loud.
"They are only for me,"
she said very proud.

Grace Anne and Nickel didn't
know what to say,
They thought Emily had come
over to play.

Then Emily carried the toys
with great care,
Down to the bedroom and
did not share.

That night, after Grace Anne
was tucked into bed,
Emily's toys kept playing
in her head.

And before she knew it, she
hopped down the stairs,
To see the toys Emily
refused to share.

The toys were so pretty,
so shiny and bright,

Grace Anne decided to take
one...NO TWO for the night!

Next morning Emily awoke and
said with a frown,
"I'm missing two toys and I am
NOT playing around!"

"Oh," whispered Grace Anne,
"I haven't seen them too."
But that wasn't the truth,
And Mother knew what to do.

"Grace Anne?" Mother asked,
in a kind but firm way,
"How would you feel if someone
took YOUR toys away?

Would you be unhappy?
Would you be mad?
Or would you be really,
really sad?

Telling the truth is sometimes
hard to do,
And now you need to tell Emily
it was you."

So Grace Anne found Emily
playing in the yard,

And thought to herself,
"This is going to be hard!"

"Emily," said Grace Anne,
"I am sorry to say,
I took your toys because I
wanted to play."

"Oh!" cried Emily,
"I was worried you see.
Thank you Grace Anne for
telling me."

"I am sorry," said Grace Anne,
"It was the wrong thing to do.
Please accept my apology
to you."

So that afternoon they
sold lemonade,
And practiced sharing and a
friendship was made.

They mixed and they stirred and
had a great day,
Even Nickel came over to play.

That night, when Grace Anne
was tucked into bed,
The lessons she learned danced
in her head.

She felt warm and cozy all
through the night,
Because she knew she did what
was right.

Grace Anne Books!

DISCUSSION PAGE: It's important for children to understand the meaning of each of these words. Use the questions below to help a child apply these words to this story and to their own lives.

G ratitude: Children should learn to show gratitude by saying, "Thank You!"

Ask: What did Emily say when Grace Anne gave back her toys? (Thank You) What is something you can share with others? Can you remember when someone shared something with you? Did you say, "Thank You"?

R espect: Children should learn how to respect the decisions of others, even when they are not happy with the choices others make.

Ask: What do we do when someone doesn't share something with us? What do we do when someone takes something of ours?

A cceptance: Children should learn to accept others differences.

Ask: How is Grace Anne different than other pups? (She has three legs) What does it mean to accept someone when they are different?

C aring: Children should learn to care about the feelings of others.

Ask: How did Emily feel when she couldn't find her toys? How do you feel when someone takes something of yours?

E ducation: Children should understand why it's important to tell the truth and to share.

Ask: How did Grace Anne feel that night after she told the truth? Why should we tell the truth? Why should we share with others?

"When Grace Anne came into our family we never knew just how much joy she would bring with her. Grace Anne lost her back right leg in an accident before her first birthday, though she never lost her zest or true spirit of life. Grace Anne is a survivor and each day is filled with adventure, enthusiasm, and wonder. She is full of personality, mischief, big smiles, and contagious happiness. She is a delight and truly as special as can be."

-Cindy Anne Duncan, Author

Visit our blog: www.graceannebooks.blogspot.com